that's SO raven

Rebel Raven

Adapted by Alice Alfonsi

Based on the television series, "That's So Raven", created by Michael Poryes and Susan Sherman

Part One is based on the episode written by Ed Evans

Part Two is based on the episode written by Dava Savel

Watch it on
DISNEY CHANNEL
abc Kids

DISNEP PRESS

VOLO

New York

Printed in the United States of America

First Edition
3 5 7 9 10 8 6 4 2

Library of Congress Control Number: 2005921953

ISBN 0-7868-3601-6

For more Disney Press fun, visit www.disneybooks.com
Visit DisneyChannel.com

that's **SO** raven

Part One

Chapter One

This is messed up, thought Eddie Thomas. The first bell hadn't even rung yet and Principal Lawler was already acting freaky.

"The nose knows," Lawler muttered to himself. The stocky, gray-haired man moved down the hall, smelling students' lockers. *Sniff, sniff, sniff . . .*

Eddie shook his head. Lawler hasn't been principal very long, he thought. Maybe the pressure is getting to him.

Standing beside Eddie, Chelsea Daniels flipped back her long, red hair. She didn't care what Lawler's problem was. The man was about to invade her *aromatic* privacy, and she was going to say something about it!

"Principal Lawler," she snapped, storming right up to him, "is someone being a little bit *nosey*?"

Lawler straightened up. "P-p-pipe down, Miss Daniels," he ordered, staring at Chelsea through his partially crossed eyes. "I am p-p-pretty p-perturbed!"

Chelsea recoiled as Lawler's spit-storm of sputtering *P*s drenched her with saliva. *Eeeww*, she thought, that is just *gross*!

Hanging back, Eddie tried not to laugh at Chelsea's mistake. She'd forgotten the First Rule of Lawler. Never stand closer than two feet from the man. His geyser of spit was as dependable as Old Faithful!

Eddie had learned this from personal experience. Back when Lawler was still teaching English, Eddie had been forced to sit in the front row. He'd silently chanted *rain, rain, go away* for an entire semester. It hadn't helped.

The spray had gotten so bad, he'd pulled garbage bags over his clothes just to keep them dry.

"The Gourmet Cooking Club is missing a very expensive, very p-p-pungent P-P-Parmesan," Lawler continued, "and I intend to *sniff* it out."

Eddie wasn't sure he'd heard right. "You mean to tell me someone jacked some *stanky* cheese?"

"P-p-precisely!" Lawler replied, spraying Chelsea like a lawn sprinkler.

"Oh, man," she whispered to Eddie as she wiped her face, "you had to ask. Why?"

"Things need to tighten up around here," Lawler declared angrily. "P-p-people come to school like it's one big p-p-party."

Chelsea was about to argue that point when her best friend, Raven Baxter, burst through the double doors at the end of the hall. "Party over here! Party over here!" Raven sang to the music blasting in her headphones.

Mr. Lawler didn't notice Raven right away. He had gone back to sniffing lockers. Unfortunately, Raven didn't notice Mr. Lawler, either. She kept bustin' moves down the hall, wildly swinging her arms, causing the huge lilac ruffles on her sleeves to sail through the air.

"Party over here! Party over here!" Raven continued to sing at the top of her lungs. She twirled three times. The matching ruffles she'd sewn into her bell-bottoms spun with her.

Chelsea and Eddie waved their hands and pointed to Lawler, who was just a few feet away, sniffing lockers. But Raven didn't notice the principal. She just waved her hands and pointed, too, imitating her friends. She figured they were doing some old dance steps.

"Jump, jump!" she cried, still grooving to

the music. "Hey, that's old school. Jump, jump!"

Finally, Mr. Lawler turned and saw Raven.

And *she* finally saw *him*.

With a gulp of dread, Raven yanked off her headphones. "Oh, hey, Mr. Lawler," she said, making her big brown eyes go wide and innocent. Out of the side of her mouth, she hissed at Eddie and Chelsea. "Why didn't y'all *tell* me it's Mr. Lawler?"

The principal cleared his throat. He narrowed his eyes at the crazy lilac ruffles on Raven's sleeves and bell-bottoms. He frowned at the flashy rhinestone choker around her neck and the glitter stars and moons on her blouse.

"Miss Baxter," Lawler said sternly, "I would appreciate it if you would dress and act appropriately."

Excuse *you*, she thought, putting her hand

on her hip. "What's wrong with the way I dress?"

Lawler raised an eyebrow. "It's *distracting* to the learning process! In fact, I'll be implementing some new policies."

What? Raven thought. She didn't like the sound of that. She was about to ask Lawler for the 411 on his so-called "new policies." But when she opened her mouth to speak, nothing came out. Her whole body began to tingle. Then her eyes glazed over and everything around her faded from view as strange new images flooded her mind. . . .

**Through her eye
The vision runs
Flash of future
Here it comes—**

I'm in the school cafeteria. I see Principal Lawler. He's standing at the front of the room beside a long table. There are piles of folded clothes on it. Kids are walking up to the table, one by one.

What is this? Some kind of charity drive? Must be. Someone's hung a wack outfit behind the table. Navy blue blazer, red tie, white shirt, plaid skirt, white knee socks. Blech! I can see why they're giving that outfit away to charity. If I had an outfit like that, I'd give it away, too!

Now Lawler's looking down at a clipboard in his hands. He's announcing something: "Come get your uniforms. Uniforms here. Come get your uniforms. Paulson, Pearman, Pfeiffer . . ."

Wait a second. This is no charity drive. Kids aren't donating their old clothes. They're being forced to take new ones! . . . Oh, now I see. There's a sign hanging behind the table. It reads: UNIFORM PICKUP.

School uniforms? At Bayside? No way! This cannot be happening!

As Raven came out of her vision, she was completely horrified. I can't let this happen, she told herself.

"Mr. Lawler," said Raven, stepping up to the principal, "you're not thinking of making everyone wear uniforms, are you?"

"I wasn't . . ." he replied, then the man tapped his cheek in thought. "But that's a splendid proposal!"

One week later, Lawler was standing on the big staircase outside the cafeteria. A crowd of students had gathered at the bottom.

"I am proud to present your new school uniforms!" the principal announced.

He turned and gestured for two students to come down the steps. The girl and boy he'd grabbed at random hadn't wanted to model the uniforms. But Lawler found that one, simple word—*suspension*—went a long way in persuading them!

With stiff steps, the reluctant models walked down to the middle of the staircase. Raven, standing in the crowd gathered below, looked up and cringed. The girl model was Chelsea! The boy model was Eddie!

Chelsea wore the same hideous outfit Raven had seen in her vision. The plaid skirt practically covered her knees—*Ugh!* The plain white blouse was a total yawn. The navy blue blazer had all the charm of a cardboard box. And the red tie looked like something a Boy Scout would wear to a jamboree.

Eddie looked even worse. He wore the exact same blue blazer and red tie as Chelsea. But instead of a skirt, he wore khaki shorts and white knee socks.

Chelsea spotted her best friend in the crowd below. "Way to go, Rae," she called unhappily.

Raven winced. "Hey, you guys. I'm sorry, okay. I was trying to *prevent* my vision from happening, but I guess I kind of . . . *made* it happen."

Eddie felt like a reject from an English boarding school. Plus, the elastic in his white socks was cutting off his circulation.

Shaking his head, he glared at Raven. *Dang,* he thought, a homeboy being forced to dress like Harry Potter? "This is just wrong."

Chapter Two

Principal Lawler herded the kids into the cafeteria. A long table was set up in the front of the room. It was piled high with folded clothes. As Lawler called out names, students walked up to receive their uniforms.

"Come get your uniforms," called Principal Lawler. "Paulson, Pearman, Pfeiffer . . ."

Raven shuddered. This is just like my vision, she realized.

"Rae, you know this is all your fault," said Chelsea, still dressed in her uniform.

"I know," she replied, turning to face Chelsea and Eddie. "But you guys didn't have to volunteer to model."

"What?" Chelsea squawked.

"Volunteer?" Eddie cried. "Rae, he threatened to put us on *suspension*."

All around them, students were grumbling. Suddenly, a girl the size of Godzilla roughly cleared a path. "Move!" cried Loca. "Alana's coming through!"

Eddie, Chelsea, and Raven jumped back fast. Alana was a loudmouth with blond highlights and an off-the-charts diva attitude. She and Raven used to be friends. And that was a big *used to*—like back in grade school.

These days, Alana thought she was "all that." She even traveled with a bad girl posse of two: the giant Loca, also known as "the enforcer," and a prissy girl named Muffy who spent most of her day telling everyone what Alana was thinking.

"Yo, Mr. Principal," said Alana, getting right up into Lawler's face. "Me and my girls already got a uniform!"

Alana waved Loca and Muffy forward. The three gave each other their special handshake of four claps, three snaps, and two slaps. Then they struck a pose in their color-coordinated outfits of the day—baby blue tracksuits.

Lawler folded his arms. "Well," he replied, "from now on you and your posse will be spending less time p-p-picking out clothes, and more time improving your p-p-pitiful grade-p-p-point averages."

Raven, Chelsea, and Eddie nearly burst out laughing when they realized Alana had forgotten the First Rule of Lawler. Every *P* he'd pronounced had soaked the girl with spittle.

As Alana stood frozen in horror, Muffy pulled out a tissue. "Excuse me, sir," Muffy snapped, blotting her leader's face. "Alana would appreciate it if you would *say* it, not *spray* it."

"I don't get your point," Lawler replied in

confusion. Then with a shrug, he turned and walked away.

Meanwhile, Eddie was still freaking over his uniform. "I never told you all this," he told Raven and Chelsea, "but I hate my knees."

"And you know what," said Raven, "you shouldn't *have* to show them."

"And we shouldn't have to look at them," added Chelsea.

"No, Chelsea, no," said Raven. "I'm saying *nobody* should *tell* us what to wear. *Right?*"

"Right!" cried a dozen kids around her.

Raven jumped. She hadn't realized kids in the crowd were listening to her. "Oh, hey, y'all," she said nervously. Then she realized more kids were gathering around. And that gave her an idea.

"No, no, listen to what I'm saying," she continued, raising her voice enough for more kids to hear, "we shouldn't all have to walk around the school looking the same. Right?"

"Right!" shouted her fellow classmates.

"So tomorrow we need to make a statement," she cried. "Yeah, sure, we'll wear the uniforms, but we'll wear 'em *our* way!"

"Right!" agreed everyone.

Raven felt inspired. Look at me, she thought. I am single-handedly leading a clothing revolution! Suddenly, her voice took on the emotion of a gospel preacher. "We will take that uniform and we will *customize*!" Raven proclaimed.

"Right!" the crowd responded.

"We will *accessorize*!" Raven declared.

"Right!" the crowd agreed.

"I'm talking about *individualize*!"

"Right!"

"*Funkification* to the highest level," Raven finally cried. "Get it? Now who's with me?"

Everyone raised their fists in the air and

cheered. Raven couldn't help grinning from ear to ear. *Dang*, she thought, I am good!

Later that day, Raven's little brother, Cory, was hanging out with his friend William. The two ten-year-olds had just finished school. They were about to look for a snack in the Baxters' kitchen when Cory noticed the pile of mail on the counter. Curious, he hopped on a stool and looked through the pile.

"How come I never get any mail?" Cory wondered aloud.

"Do you ever write anybody?" asked William.

Cory shook his head. "Nope."

"Well," said William, "there you go."

"Hey, look," said Cory, holding up one of the letters. "This one's for Lionel."

Lionel was Cory's pet. At the moment, the little black-and-white rodent was perched on his shoulder. "You're a rat," Cory told Lionel. "I know you never wrote anybody."

Cory scratched his head. He checked the address again, just to be sure. It said *Lionel* Baxter, all right. Which was totally weird. Whoever heard of a rat getting mail? he thought as he tore open the envelope. Other than my sister, Raven, of course!

"Whoa!" cried Cory, when he saw the plastic card inside the envelope. "Look, it's a credit card!"

William checked out the contents and nodded. It was a credit card, all right, and Lionel's name was written on it. William wasn't exactly sure how credit cards worked, but he *was* sure of one thing. "My parents use them when they don't have money."

"Lionel doesn't have any money," said Cory. Then he held up the card. "But he does now," he realized. "*Cha-ching!*"

The next morning, Raven excitedly burst through the front doors of Bayside. "Today's the day, people!" she shouted at the top of her lungs. "It's protest day!"

Raven was proud of the way she'd *customized, accessorized,* and *funkified* her school uniform. First, she'd shortened her standard-issue knee-length skirt to make the lame pleated plaid look modern. Next, she'd embroidered her blazer's dull navy lapels with glitter and rhinestones. Then, she'd slapped three silver chain belts around her hips, sewed a feather boa onto her red tie, and rolled her white socks down to her bright red high-tops.

Oooooh, she thought, it feels so good to be a fashionista freedom fighter! "Let's stand up and be counted!" Raven cried to her classmates. She raised her hand. "One!"

She waited for her fellow Bayside Barracudas to sound off and show her what wild and crazy things they'd done to their uniforms. But they didn't.

Every last student staring at her in the packed hallway was wearing their standard-issue rags. Every crease was in place, every blazer pressed, every white knee sock pulled up, and every leather loafer polished.

Oh, no, she thought. I am *not* seeing this. Raven panicked. She raced through the sea of navy blazers, pleated skirts, and red ties—all perfectly knotted.

"Isn't anyone going to help me out here?" she cried. "Can I get an untucked shirt? Can I get some saggy pants? Work with me, people!"

With guilty looks, students slunk away from Raven and headed off to class. Finally, Raven saw a friendly face.

"Wow, you look fantastic!" Chelsea cried.

"Thank you, thank you. I know I do," said Raven, spinning to show off her funkified uniform. Then she looked at Chelsea's uniform and asked, "How come *you* don't?"

Knee-length skirt, stupid red tie, ridiculous white socks, Raven cataloged to herself as she looked Chelsea over. Not one piece of her uniform was missing, changed, or out of place.

Chelsea swallowed uncomfortably. "Right, right, the protest," she said nervously. "Funny story . . . thought about it . . . bad idea."

Raven already had guessed why the other students hadn't protested. Principal Lawler had sent letters home with the students, telling them how to wear their uniforms—and how *not* to wear them. Any student caught violating the rules would be sent to detention. Raven had been willing to risk it. And she thought her best friends were, too.

"Why didn't you call me, Chels?" Raven asked.

"Again . . . thought about it. Bad idea," Chelsea replied guiltily. "You know, I'm sorry, Rae. . . . I thought you'd be mad."

"Really?" Raven asked.

"Yeah," said Chelsea.

Raven exploded. "How do you think I feel now?"

"Oh, come on," said Chelsea, throwing up her hands. "That's just the kind of reaction I was hoping to avoid."

Just then, Raven noticed Eddie walking up to them. His knobby knees were in plain sight—along with his pristine standard uniform. Raven couldn't believe Eddie had let her down, too.

"And what's your excuse, Li'l Nasty Knees?" she snapped.

Eddie shrugged. "Chelsea called and told me it was off."

"Yes and *he* took it very well," Chelsea pointed out. "That's all I'm saying."

"You know, the whole school wimped out on me! That's a shame," Raven said. But what hurt her the most were the two people standing in front of her. "And my best friends didn't have my back!"

"Miss Baxter!" a voice called from down the hall.

Oh, snap! Here we go, thought Raven as Principal Lawler stormed up to her.

"What you've done to your uniform is p-p-prohibited!" the man shouted.

"I know," said Raven. Then she gathered her courage and faced the principal. "But, Mr. Lawler, I don't think it's fair that we should be told what to wear. Okay, this is a protest." She glanced around at the empty hallway and sighed. "The world's *loneliest* protest."

"Well, you can protest in detention," Lawler declared.

Raven didn't know whether she felt more furious than hurt—or more hurt than furious. Either way, the source of her pain wasn't Principal Lawler. As he marched her away, she tossed a final disappointed glance at her so-called friends.

"Good looking out, guys," she whispered to Chelsea and Eddie. They both looked distressed, but neither one knew what to say.

Chapter Three

When Raven walked into the detention room, the teacher barely looked up from his newspaper. The room was almost full. Only one chair was vacant on the row at the end, and Raven dejectedly plopped into it.

The three girls in the seats around Raven turned. Uh-oh, she thought, seeing Alana, Muffy, and the giant "enforcer," Loca!

"Ow, ow, ow, ow, ow!" Raven automatically cried.

Loca rolled her eyes. "I haven't even touched you."

"I'm just practicing," said Raven. After all, she figured it was just a matter of time before Alana ordered Loca to turn her into a pretzel. "Ow, ow, ow, ow . . ."

But Alana waved her hand. "Don't worry, Baxter," she said, "we're not going to mess you up."

That's when Raven took a closer look at Alana and her posse. All three girls had jazzed up their school uniforms. Alana and Muffy had sewn zebra-print fringe on the lapels of their blazers and wore bright red tights instead of those awful knee socks. Loca wore sweatpants beneath her pleated skirt, and on her head sat a red Kangol cap.

Dang, thought Raven, these girls actually heeded my call to customize and accessorize. It was a true example of funkification.

"You guys joined my protest!" Raven cried with joy.

Alana nodded. "It looks like *we're* the only ones in this school to have any *guts.*"

Raven sighed. "All I know is my two best

friends didn't even back me up and you guys did."

"Yeah," said Loca in disgust, "they dogged you out."

"Straight left you hangin'," Alana agreed.

Muffy's head bobbed up and down. "Nice friends. *Not.*"

Alana looked Raven up and down. "You know what, Baxter?" she said. "You're not as big of a spineless punk as I thought you were."

Raven smiled. "Stop it. You're going to give me a big head." On the other hand, she thought, I am having a pretty sour day. A little more sugar couldn't hurt. "Okay," she told Alana, "keep it coming."

Alana waved her girls closer. "Now let's go cause some trouble."

"What?" Raven tensed. Alana, Muffy, and Loca stared, and Raven realized she was out-numbered. "Oh, okay," she said nervously.

"Just want you to know, I'm kind of new at this, so I'm thinking we should start off with *mischief* and work our way up."

Loca narrowed her eyes. "Here's how it works, they mess us up, and we mess them up."

Raven gulped. "*Them*, meaning . . . ?"

"Principal Lawler. He's going to *p-p-pay*!" Alana cried, imitating Lawler's exploding *P*s.

Loca, Muffy, and Alana all laughed.

Raven didn't.

Alana glared at Raven, and Muffy tapped her on the shoulder—*hard.* "When Alana laughs," Muffy said, "the whole world laughs *with* her."

Raven's eyes widened. "Ha, ha, ha! Ha, ha, ha!" she cried. Suddenly everyone stopped laughing. Raven didn't notice. "Ha, ha, ha! Ha, ha, ha!" she continued.

Alana glared. Muffy tapped Raven again. "And when Alana *stops* . . ."

Raven gulped. "Right, sorry."

"Okay," said Alana, "now, check this out!" She snapped her fingers. Loca reached into her gym bag and pulled out a thick disclike object about twelve inches across. It was covered in paper, and it took Raven a second to realize what it was—the big, expensive wheel of Parmesan cheese.

"Oh, my goodness!" Raven cried. "You guys found the missing cheese!"

Alana and Muffy lunged forward to cover Raven's mouth.

"You guys stole the missing cheese?" Raven whispered nervously when they finally removed their hands. "Tight."

"And you're never going to guess what we're going to do with it," said Alana with an evil little grin.

Suddenly, Raven felt that familiar tingle again. Her head began to spin and her eyes glazed over. Then everything around her seemed to freeze in time. . . .

Through her eye
The vision runs
Flash of future
Here it comes—

Whoa, what is this place? Looks like I'm in a tunnel lined with aluminum. Okay, either I'm crawling in the school's heating ducts or I've been shrunk down to rodent size and shoved into a hamster habitat.

Wait, there's something up ahead. It's that wheel of stinky Parmesan cheese. The heat from the school is on. I can feel it underneath me. And it's melting the cheese. Oh, nasty! The thing is bubbling and oozing and sending out waves of nuclear level stank!

Raven shuddered as she came out of her

vision. That messed-up cheese stink was still in her nostrils.

Maybe I can talk her out of this, Raven thought.

"Um, Alana . . ." she began nervously. "Hey, girl. You're not thinking of putting that cheese in a vent and, you know, letting it get all hot and stinky and bubbly and stinkin' up the whole school, are you?"

Muffy shook her head. "No," she replied. "Alana was going to grate it over some angel hair pasta."

"But we like your idea so much better!" Alana squealed.

Raven was horrified. "No, no, no!" she cried. "It wasn't my idea. I was just saying it because I thought that's what your evil minds were going to do. So I'm really sorry I—"

Raven stopped talking. She had to. Alana

had just reached out her hand and squeezed her lips shut.

"Baxter, you talk too much," Alana said. Then a nasty smile spread across her face. "But you're an evil genius."

"Thank you," Raven said when Alana finally let go of her lips.

"All right now," Alana told her crew, "this uniform thing stinks and tomorrow, thanks to Raven, the whole school's going to stink!"

Alana put her hand out. Loca put her hand on top of Alana's. Muffy put her hand on top of Loca's. Then they all stared at Raven, waiting for her hand to join theirs.

Muffy smirked. "Alana feels if you have a hand, you should put it in."

Raven shook her head. I can't go along with this, she thought. I've got to stand up to them. But how?

"Hey, guys," she tried, "I'm really going

to think about it. Maybe sleep on it?"

Loca frowned at Raven. A second later, Godzilla Girl grabbed Raven's hand and shoved it on top of Alana's.

Raven furrowed her brow. "Okay, well, I'm in there with you," she said with a fearful glance at Loca.

Loca nodded her approval. And Raven forced a smile. I can't believe they're going forward with their nasty little plan, she thought. And I'm such a wimp! I'm not even going to stop them.

All of a sudden, Raven felt stankier than the wheel of Parmesan.

After school that day, Loca went looking for Raven. She found her at her locker and walked her down the hall. Muffy and Alana were already waiting around the corner from the school's main heating vent.

When Alana saw that they were all assembled, she poked Muffy in the ribs. The girl peeked around the corner and whispered. "Okay, the coast is, like, clear."

A few minutes later, the human tower was in place. Muffy handed the cheese up to Loca. "Whoa," Loca said, "this is some serious *stank*." She then passed the cheese up to Alana, who was sitting on Loca's shoulders.

"This is just beautiful," said Alana, teetering on top of Loca.

Alana pulled open the grate covering the heating vent. Inside was a complex network of aluminum-lined ducts. Each duct led to a vent in every classroom at Bayside.

Alana shoved the big wheel of expensive Parmesan through the vent and into the aluminum duct. "Okay, the cheese is in the vent," she said, smiling with satisfaction. "Tomorrow, when they turn on the heat, this school is going to reek!"

Still holding Alana, Loca laughed. "What do you think of that?" she called down to the girl beneath her feet.

That girl was Raven. I wanted to be a fashion rebel, she silently moaned, not a human step stool! "This bad-girl stuff's a little hard on the back!"

Chapter Four

Later that day, Raven's father heard the doorbell ring. When he answered the door, he found a man in a brown uniform holding a small package.

"Delivery," said the man.

Mr. Baxter took the package. "I know what that is," he said excitedly. "My birthday's next week and I bet my wife got me that watch I've been hinting about!" He smiled at the deliveryman. "Right, right?"

The man rolled his eyes as he gave Mr. Baxter a form to sign. "I just *deliver*'em, sir."

Mr. Baxter signed the form and brought the package inside. I know I should wait for my birthday to open this, he thought. But presents are my weakness. I just can't wait!

With eager hands, he tore open the box and pulled out—a tiny, black leather jacket. Hold on, he thought, this doesn't look like an obscenely expensive *watch* to me.

Confused, he checked the address label on the box. "Mr. Lionel Baxter . . . *Lionel*?"

Shaking his head, Mr. Baxter headed for the stairs. Last time I checked, Lionel was a twitchy little rat, he thought. But his *owner* is a scheming little boy. Which means I'd better get to the bottom of this right now!

Inside Cory's bedroom, life was *good*. "Ever since Lionel got his credit card, we are livin' large!" Cory exclaimed.

Across the room, William nodded in agreement. He was sitting at Cory's desk, tapping on his *brand-new* laptop computer. Cory was lounging in his *brand-new* recliner, wearing his *brand-new* silk robe, and leafing through his stack of *brand-new* comic books. All of this stuff was courtesy of Lionel, of course, and his *brand-new* credit card.

Lionel himself no longer slept in a stinky cage. He now lived in a little rat mansion. He had his own little leather couch, tiny pillows, and bedroom furniture, too. Okay, thought Cory, so it's really a dollhouse, but Lionel doesn't know the difference!

Suddenly, Cory heard his bedroom door opening. His father walked in and held up Lionel's latest purchase.

"Cory," Mr. Baxter began, "why does Lionel have a little leather jacket?"

Cory shrugged. He thought it was obvious. "So he can look cool on his little motorcycle!" Cory held up the little rat-sized motorcycle he'd bought two days before.

Mr. Baxter started looking around the

room. He saw the new recliner, the robe, the comics, the dollhouse, the computer, and a pile of video games on the floor. He also saw an electric guitar, a model plane, and a pile of new toys. "Son, where did all this stuff come from?"

Cory smiled with pride. "Nice, huh? My man William ordered it all from the Internet. Life is good."

Mr. Baxter frowned. "Is life still going to be good when I find out how you *paid* for it?"

"That's the beauty of it," said Cory, waving his hand. "It's all on the card." With a snap of his fingers, Cory commanded William to show off Lionel's very own credit card.

Mr. Baxter grabbed the piece of plastic and read it. He couldn't believe his eyes. "They gave a credit card to a *rat*?" Then he realized something even worse. "It's platinum. Even I can't get a platinum card!" Mr. Baxter smacked his forehead. Clearly, the credit card company had made a monumental error. He turned to Cory. "Do you know how credit cards work?"

Cory smirked. "Obviously," he said, waving at the stuff he'd recently purchased.

Mr. Baxter sighed. "Cory, when you use a credit card, you can buy stuff with it *now*, but *someone* has to pay for it *later*."

"Who's that someone going to be?" Cory asked. He honestly wanted to know.

Mr. Baxter folded his arms. He was sorry to deliver the bad news. "It's going to be *you*."

"Me?" Cory cried, jumping out of his brand-new recliner. "I can't afford all this stuff."

"Now you get it," said Mr. Baxter, heading for the door. "That's why all this stuff has to go back!"

Cory shook his head and thought, I knew it was too good to be true. Then again, when it comes to paying the bills, nobody does it better than dear old Dad!

"Okay," Cory called to his father, "we're sorry. We didn't know. I guess we've got to give back your *birthday present*, too."

Mr. Baxter froze in the hall. Birthday presents were his weakness—and Cory knew it. "You got me a little somethin', somethin'?" he asked, stepping back into the room. He glanced around with open curiosity.

Just then, everyone heard a familiar sound coming from outside. *Jingle, jingle, jingle . . .*

Mr. Baxter's eyes brightened. "You got me an ice-cream truck?"

Cory smiled. "Always thinking of you, Dad."

Mr. Baxter sighed. "You know this stuff has got to go back."

"I know," Cory said sadly.

Jingle, jingle, jingle . . .

"Right after we get our fudgey pops!" cried Mr. Baxter. Then William, Cory, and his father all raced out the door.

The next day at school, Raven got a whole new attitude—a bad one.

Alana, Muffy, and Loca had all dressed in their regulation school uniforms. They'd added only one extra thing to their outfits, superdiva sunglasses. They met Raven at her locker and handed her a pair. Raven slipped them on. Alana snapped her fingers and told Raven she looked fly.

Suddenly, Raven *felt* fly—even in her stupid school uniform. She joined Alana, Muffy, and Loca as they strutted down the hallway together. Their bad attitude was broadcasting large and in charge. When kids saw them coming, they backed away, giving them room to pass.

One boy moved too slowly. Alana took off her sunglasses and stared him down. Raven imitated her along with Muffy and Loca. The kid backed away with total dread. Alana snapped her fingers again, and the girls continued their strut.

Dang, thought Raven, I've never been *bad* before. I didn't know it could feel so *good*!

"Raven?" called a familiar voice.

Raven turned to find Chelsea standing by the water fountain. "Chelsea?" said Raven.

Chelsea had backed up against the wall to let Alana, Loca, and Muffy pass. She looked stunned to see that Raven had joined Alana's sunglasses posse.

Just then, Eddie walked up. "Raven, Chelsea . . ."

Now Loca stopped. "Eddie!" she cried with delight. She'd had a little crush on him not long ago, but now they were just good friends. The big girl gave him a playful punch.

The punch didn't feel very playful to Eddie, however. Godzilla Girl packed a real wallop, and Eddie cringed in pain. "Loca," he squeaked, rubbing his arm.

Alana was freaked by all this meeting and greeting. "Muffy!" she cried.

Muffy leaped forward. "Alana feels the name thing should stop," she quickly declared, "like, *now*."

"Excuse me," said Chelsea, pulling Raven aside. "Raven, a word."

Eddie joined their tight huddle.

"Rae," whispered Chelsea in alarm, "why are you hanging out with *them*?"

"Okay," snapped Raven, "unlike some people, when they say they're going to do something, they actually come through."

Eddie scratched his head. "Rae, you still trippin' off the uniform thing?"

Raven harrumphed in his face. "At least my girls got my biz-zack!"

Chelsea put her hands on her hips. "I cannot believe you're actually dropping us just because we weren't down with your stupid protest."

"Oh," said Raven, "now it's stupid?"

Eddie sighed. "It was stupid then, too, Rae."

"You guys *were* cheering for me," she reminded them. "What were you thinking?"

"W-well, I d-don't know, Rae," Chelsea sputtered, "sometimes it's hard to think and cheer at the same time!"

"When a friend is counting on you, you shouldn't *have* to think," Raven pointed out.

Chelsea and Eddie exchanged guilty looks. They knew Raven was right.

"Raven, you coming?" called Loca.

Raven glanced back and forth between her two sets of friends. It didn't take long for her to make a decision. "Yo," she called to Loca, "be right there, skillet home biscuit."

As Raven turned and headed off, Chelsea and Eddie stared after her with open mouths. They couldn't believe it. Their girl had turned gangsta.

"Man," Chelsea finally said, "it's always hard to watch a good girl go biz-zad."

Chapter Five

"Loca . . . Time?" Alana asked with a snap of her fingers.

Loca glanced at her watch. "The heat comes on in two minutes."

Alana looked around and grinned. "Yep, this school is going to smell *foul*. Now, all we have to do is get rid of the cheese wrappers."

Alana pulled the Parmesan wheel's wrappers out of her backpack. Suddenly, Raven froze.

Through her eye
The vision runs
Flash of future
Here it comes—

I'm seeing Alana with those Parmesan cheese wrappers in her hands. But what's she doing with them?

Hmmm . . . looks like trouble. She's glancing around to make sure no one is watching her. Now she's shoving pieces of those wrappers into two lockers. . . . Wait a second, those lockers look awfully familiar to me. . . .

"One for Eddie," Alana says with a giggle. "One for Chelsea!"

Oh, no! Those lockers belong to Eddie and Chelsea! Alana is trying to frame my best friends!

As Raven came out of her vision, she thought, I've got to put a stop to this. She turned to Alana. "Hey, you're not thinking of putting the cheese wrappers in Eddie and Chelsea's lockers, trying to frame them, are you?"

"No, we were just going to put them in the

trash," Alana replied. Then her eyes widened in delight. "But we like *your* idea *so* much better!"

Ugh, thought Raven, I did it again! "Listen," she quickly told Alana, "my friends had nothing to do with it."

"Oh, I know," Alana replied with an evil grin. "You are cold, girl. I love it!"

"Here comes the heat," Loca announced. She pointed down the hall.

Raven turned to see the school's custodian adjusting the thermostat. Together, Alana, Muffy, and Loca giggled and put on their nose plugs. Then Alana held up the incriminating cheese wrappers and smiled at her crew. "Let's get framin', girls!" she cried and led the way to Chelsea and Eddie's lockers.

Raven didn't follow. Chelsea and Eddie may have let me down, she thought, but I'm not down with revenge. No way. Seeing them get burned is the last thing I want.

Raven had to do something. But what?

She raced over to the thermostat. The easiest way to stop the cheese from *stinking* is to stop it from *melting*, she decided. And the easiest way to stop it from *melting* is to stop the school's furnace from coming on.

But the custodian had replaced the box of unbreakable glass around the thermostat and secured it with a padlock. There was no way for Raven to turn off the heat.

"It's locked!" she cried, pulling at the padlock on the thermostat. "Arrrgh! . . . I've *got* to stop that cheese."

What now? she asked herself. She glanced across the hall and found her answer. A boy stood beside a bank of lockers. He looked as tall as a skyscraper with shoulders as wide as a tabletop.

Now that's what I'm talkin' about, Raven thought. "Hey, Stretch!" she called to the basketball team's center. "I need a lift, man!"

Stretch smiled down at Raven. A few minutes later, he was lifting her up to the school's main heating vent.

"Thanks, Stretch," she called, "this is my floor!"

Raven pulled off the grate that covered the vent's opening. She peered inside. A long network of aluminum ducts stretched off into the darkness. Whoa, she thought, good thing this wheel of cheese is close to the opening.

"Okay," she mumbled, seeing the Parmesan sitting right in front of her. "Little cheezy is comin' home with me."

Raven reached for the cheese, but it was sitting a little too far away. Her fingers could only brush its surface. "Stretch, I'm sorry," she called down to her human elevator. "A little higher. Okay? Higher."

Raven *really* stretched this time. She could

feel her arm muscles straining, her fingers reaching. She levered the cheese wheel up on its side to get a good grip. She *almost* had it. But it suddenly rolled away!

Raven watched in horror as the thick, creamy wheel of expensive Parmesan traveled down the long vent. A second later, it disappeared into the darkness.

"It had to be a *wheel* of cheese," she griped. Then she called down one more time to the boy below her. "Hey, Stretch? Can you get me even *higher*?"

With one final boost, Raven climbed all the way into the vent's narrow opening. Taking a deep breath for courage, she began to crawl after the cheese.

I cannot believe I'm doing this, she thought, moving through the tunnel of aluminum. But there was no other way to retrieve the cheese, prevent the stink, and save her friends from suspension or worse—expulsion.

"Oh, dead bugs, dead bugs!" Raven cried. She shuddered and increased the speed of her crawl. Then she was totally *over* those dead bugs. And for a very good reason—

"Live bugs. Live, live, *live* bugs!" she cried, then stopped. She had come to an intersection of ducts. She could go forward, turn right, or turn left. "Which way?" she wondered. The faintest wisp of cheese stink hit her nose. "*Definitely* this way," she decided and rounded the corner to the left.

"Whoa, I'm hot!" Raven complained. She could already feel the heat coming through the vents. She peeled off her navy blazer and continued crawling. Then she took a hair band from her wrist and pulled back her hair.

As she moved forward, the cheese smell became overwhelming. She peered into the darkness and moved another few feet. Finally, she saw it. "There you are, ya nasty!" she cried. "Come to mama!"

Raven quickly crawled toward the cheese, but actually *getting* to the stinky wheel wasn't as easy as it looked. The farther Raven crawled, the narrower the aluminum duct became.

"Oh, man," Raven complained, "it's getting kind of small."

Raven's arms became pinned to her sides and she wiggled toward the cheese like a worm. Finally, the vent became so narrow, she could only get her head through.

"I can't move my arms!" she complained.

She wiggled as close to the cheese as she could. Now her face was right next to the wheel. It really was nasty—melting and bubbling from the heat. Even if she could have gotten her arms free and reached for it, she doubted she could have picked it up. The goo would have just slid through her fingers.

She sighed. I've come so far. There's got to be a solution. "Okay, what do I do?" she asked herself. "How do I get rid of it?"

An answer finally came to her—a terrible answer. But it was the only idea she could think of, so, with a sigh, she mumbled, "Sorry, stomach."

Raven took a deep breath, wriggled just a little closer, and lowered her mouth into the stinky, bubbling cheese. She started to eat the melting wheel like a contestant in a pie-eating contest.

If this were spread on some pizza dough, I'd be down with it, she thought. But eating it this way . . . it's *nasty*!

"Oh, the horror," she muttered, lifting her face. The bubbling, gooey cheese dripped from her chin. Gross! she thought. But she wasn't going to quit now. Taking another deep breath, she dove back in.

Meanwhile, in the hallway just below Raven, Alana was tiptoeing up to a bank of lockers. With her nose plug still in place, she giggled as she shoved the folded cheese wrappers through the vents in the locker doors.

"One for Eddie," she said, just like in Raven's vision, "and one for Chelsea!"

"Hey," cried Eddie, storming up to Alana, "what are you doing at our lockers?"

"You're about to find out right now," she replied.

Muffy waved at the man striding down the hallway. "Excuse me, Principal Lawler," she called. "Alana has some cheese-related information."

Lawler nodded. "Ah, the p-p-pilfered P-P-Parmesan." He walked over to Alana. "Proceed."

"If you're wondering why it smells, like, a little funky up in here," said Alana, pointing to the nose plug on her face. "It's Chelsea and Eddie!"

Lawler sniffed the air. "I don't smell anything."

Alana, Loca, and Muffy exchanged glances. Cautiously, they removed their nose plugs and sniffed.

"Me neither," said Loca.

Muffy nodded. "Something *doesn't* stink."

Alana narrowed her eyes. "Oh, something stinks all right." She turned to Eddie and Chelsea. "Where's Raven?"

In the ceiling vent right above them, Raven was trying not to hurl. Disgusted and exhausted, she had eaten almost every bit of the bubbling cheese wheel. There was only one small morsel left.

She closed her eyes and told herself, "One more bite and it's over. It's all over." Finally, with the melted cheese all over her cheeks and chin, Raven opened her mouth and sucked in the very last bite.

Crack . . . crack . . . crack!

Raven panicked as she realized the ceiling below her was starting to break. She began to wriggle her way out of the heating duct, but her movements only weakened the ceiling more.

Crrraaaaaaaack!

Suddenly, the whole thing gave way. The duct broke open, and the ceiling crumbled.

Crash!

In the hall below, Alana, Muffy, Loca, Chelsea, Eddie, and Principal Lawler all leaped backward.

Dang, Eddie thought. The weatherman was wrong this morning. He said we'd have a clear, cloudless day with no precipitation. But from where I'm standing, it's raining Ravens!

Chapter Six

Eddie shook his head at the sight of his best friend. She was lying flat on her stomach, her mouth and chin covered with funky-smelling goo. "Rae, Rae, Rae, Rae. . . ." he chanted.

Okay, Raven thought, so I've just crawled through a filthy heating vent, stuffed myself with stinky cheese, and fallen through the school ceiling. Does that mean I can't look presentable? She quickly stood up and brushed herself off. "So, how y'all doing?"

The principal looked at Raven and frowned. "Miss Baxter, dropping from the ceiling is strictly prohibited."

Loca put a hand on her hip and glared. "Where's the cheese, Baxter?"

Raven tried for the wide-eyed, innocent look. "What cheese?"

Loca folded her arms and pointed to Raven's face. *Whoops!* Raven thought as she quickly swiped the gooey mess away with her shirttail.

Alana charged forward and got in her face. "Look," she said, forgetting that Lawler was standing right behind her, "we did not steal that cheese for you to mess up our plan."

"*You* stole the cheese?" the principal said, outraged.

Alana panicked.

Loca froze.

And Muffy freaked. "Alana can't believe she said that out loud!"

Raven shook her head. "No, no, Mr. Lawler, listen. I just want you to know that Eddie and Chelsea had nothing to do with this. Okay, it was my idea to put the cheese in the vent, then I had to get it out before it stunk up the whole school and you blamed it on my friends."

Chelsea and Eddie shared guilty glances. Both of them felt terrible. They had bailed on Raven when she needed them. Yet Raven had risked her neck to keep them out of trouble. If that wasn't a genuine act of friendship, they didn't know what was.

The principal, however, remained unimpressed. "Very touching," he said, but his tone said *not*! "Now the p-p-perpetrator's p-p-parents will be hearing from me about their punishment," he warned. "And you, Miss Baxter, p-p-prepare for detention."

Eddie stepped up. "Oh, no, wait a minute. None of this would've happened if we would've backed Raven up in the first place."

"Yeah," Chelsea agreed, stepping up with him.

"Now if *she* goes to detention, *we're* going with her!" Eddie cried. He looked around at

Chelsea and Eddie showed off the
new required school uniforms.

"We will take that uniform, and we will
customize!" Raven proclaimed.

"Hey, look," said Cory, holding up one of the letters. "This one's for Lionel."

"You know, the whole school wimped out on me! That's a shame," Raven said. "And my best friends didn't have my back!"

Uh-oh, Raven thought, as she walked
into detention and noticed Alana,
Muffy, and the giant "enforcer," Loca!

"Ever since Lionel got his credit card, we
are livin' large!" Cory exclaimed.

"Actually, I think I'm more one of them," Raven said, putting her arms around her old friends.

"Fab-u-lous!" Raven cried.

"I'm just a simple girl with a private jet..."
Raven and Chelsea belted out.

"Oh, man," Cory yelped as Eddie and Chelsea dumped mashed potatoes down his pants.

"Hello," said Raven in a soft, breathy voice.
"I am the yoga teacher."

"Look! Free protein shakes!" Raven shouted
at the muscle-bound crew chasing her.

"Oh, snap!" Raven cried. "*I'm* the creep."

"Oh, that's my stomach growling,"
Mrs. Baxter lied as she patted her tummy.

"No, they are *rubbing* me the wrong way! I've got to get out of these pants!" Cory cried.

"You should come to my gardening club," Mrs. Baxter said. "It's radish week!"

the crowd of students that had gathered. "Now who's with me?"

Chelsea shook her fist in the air. "I am!" she cried. Then she and Eddie waited for cheers of support.

They never came.

The crowd of kids murmured among themselves for a second, then hurried away.

Eddie couldn't believe his classmates were so spineless. "Y'all the worst crowd ever!" he shouted after them.

Chelsea didn't care. Let them be wimps, she thought, facing the principal. "Detention for three, please," she declared.

"I'll p-p-prepare the p-p-paperwork, p-p-pronto!" he replied.

Chelsea wiped the spit off her face. *Yuck*, she thought. Detention I don't mind. It's being given a "shower" I can't stand!

After Lawler strode away, Alana walked up

to Raven. "Yo, Baxter," she said, patting Raven on the back, "thanks for not ratting us out. Guess you're still one of us."

Raven shook her head and crossed to stand with Chelsea and Eddie. "Actually, I think I'm more one of them," she said, putting her arms around her old friends.

For the briefest second, Alana looked devastated. But then she began to laugh—really hard.

Muffy bit her lip. "Alana's laughing to hide her pain," she told Raven.

Suddenly, Alana stopped laughing. She glared at Muffy, who gulped and quickly added, "Or maybe, she just thought it was funny!"

Alana jerked her head, and her crew gathered around. With four claps, three snaps, and two slaps, the bad girls shared their special handshake. Then they all put on their matching sunglasses, wheeled on their heels, and strutted down the hall.

Raven tapped her chin. She had to admit, that handshake *did* look fly. "Maybe we need one of those," she told her friends.

Raven held out her fist. Eddie and Chelsea bumped it with each of theirs. Then with a series of slamming stomps, rhythmic claps, and final slaps, they executed the most amazing, coordinated shake they'd ever tried.

Raven and Chelsea stared at each other in total amazement. Eddie just laughed. "Yeah, like we'll ever be able to do *that* again!"

The next morning, Raven charged downstairs and into the kitchen. Cory was at the table eating his cereal. Her father was at the stove frying eggs. And her mother was standing at the counter reading a letter.

"Got to go, late, late, late!" she called to her family.

First, she'd slept in. Then, she'd had trouble finding all the pieces of her official school uniform—white knee socks, white shirt (tucked in), plaid skirt, red tie, and saddle shoes. The outfit had more parts than one of Cory's model planes.

At the counter, Mrs. Baxter tried to get her daughter to slow down. "Raven, you got a letter from your school—" she began, waving a piece of paper.

"Mom, it's the ceiling," Raven said, cutting her mother off. "I told you I'll pay for the whole thing."

From behind his cereal bowl, Cory had only one piece of advice. "Don't use a credit card!"

"*Okay!*" Raven replied. "Gotta run! Love ya!"

Before Mrs. Baxter could stop her, Raven

had grabbed a piece of toast and rushed out the door.

"I just thought you'd want to know!" Mrs. Baxter called. "The school board overruled the principal and they canceled the school uniforms!"

But it was too late. Raven was gone.

When she burst through the school's front door, she had less than five minutes to get to homeroom. But instead of racing down the hall, she froze in her tracks. Every last student in the school was wearing civilian clothes. The only one wearing a dorky uniform was Raven!

"What?" she cried and closed her eyes. Maybe this is just one of my wack psychic visions, she thought. But it wasn't. When she opened her eyes, the scene was the same.

No way, she thought. I am *not* going through an entire day as the only student dressed like this.

She checked her watch, but it was way too late to rush home and change. "Okay, you know what?" she told herself. "I can make this happen. . . ."

She charged into the crowd of kids. It's obvious I'm a fashion victim, she told herself. But a few little *donations* should make things right.

"It's cold in here," she told a passing boy wearing a bright red scarf, "you don't need that . . ."

She snatched the scarf, threw it on, and kept moving.

"Girl, I love that hat," she told another student. "It'll look even better on *me*. . . ."

Raven grabbed the hat and plopped it onto her own head. Finally, she saw a classmate wearing sunglasses. "Girl, you do not need these inside. Trust me, I do!"

Raven shoved the cool glasses onto her nose

and continued strutting down the hall. Tomorrow she'd give back the "donations." But today, she just couldn't help herself.

What can I say? It's my fate, Raven thought as she worked her look with the flip of her scarf. The fashionista in me just will not settle for less than . . . "Fab-u-lous!"

that's SO raven

Part Two

Chapter One

"**A**ll right, work it out, Rae!" Chelsea cried.

"Work it out," echoed Raven into her hairbrush.

The two girls were dancing and singing to Maisha's latest number-one hit. Raven spun and struck a pose just like her favorite pop diva. Then she and Chelsea belted out the chorus. *"I'm just a simple girl with a private jet . . ."*

Raven winked at the Maisha poster on her wall, touched her orange Maisha-style bucket hat, and did the Maisha strut across her attic bedroom. My girl's got it goin' on, she thought. If only I could meet her, my life would be complete!

"You know, this is my favorite Maisha song

ever!" Chelsea shouted over the blaring music.

"There's only one problem with it," Raven yelled. "It's not *loud* enough!"

Raven pumped up the volume on her CD player until the bass made the walls vibrate. Then Chelsea and Raven added to the thunder by stomping their feet.

It took less than sixty seconds for Mrs. Baxter to climb the stairs. "Rae!" she called, walking into her daughter's bedroom. "Rae!"

But Mrs. Baxter's words were swallowed by the music. Raven and Chelsea kept dancing and screeching. *"But I'm still Maisha from up the street!"*

With a frustrated sigh, Mrs. Baxter crossed to the CD player and hit the POWER button. Raven and Chelsea were so shocked by the sudden end to their Maisha party, they stumbled to a stop and crashed into each other.

"Raven!" cried Mrs. Baxter one more time.

Chelsea blinked, surprised to see Raven's mother in the room. Whoa, she thought, where did she come from? "Hello, Mrs. B," she said. "Great song, huh?"

Mrs. Baxter tapped the side of her head. "I'll let you know when my ears stop ringing."

Then Raven's mom studied the two girls for a moment. "Did you girls ever think about turning off the music and just enjoying some peace and quiet?"

Raven glanced at Chelsea. There was only one reply to Mrs. Baxter's question. "No!" the girls declared together.

"Well, Raven," Mrs. Baxter said, "if you change your mind, maybe you and I could have a weekend relaxing and meditating at the Silent Gardens Health Spa."

Meditating? Raven thought. With my mother? Sorry, but that is just *not* on my list of things to do for the weekend.

"Doesn't that sound like fun?" Mrs. Baxter asked with an excited smile.

"Mom," said Raven as gently as she could, "I really don't think *fun* means what *you* think it means."

Mrs. Baxter hid her disappointment behind a shrug. "Well," she said, heading for the door, "I'm going this weekend, so if you change your mind . . ."

After her mother left, Raven shuddered. I love my mom, she thought, but spending an entire weekend eating tofu and sitting in a mud bath? "Not gonna happen!" she cried.

"No," agreed Chelsea.

Suddenly, Raven was in the mood for another Maisha CD. She looked over the dozen jewel cases stacked on her dresser and chose an old favorite—one from last year. But as she glanced at the cover, Raven suddenly froze.

Through her eye
The vision runs
Flash of future
Here it comes—

I hear music with tinkling bells and whispering flutes—the stuff tofu-eating, yoga types like to play. New Age or Zen or something? Oh, and look, there's a tranquil indoor garden to go with the music. Flowers, potted palms, trickling fountains, and delicate sculptures.

For some reason, I'm seeing the whole thing upside down. But I don't get it. Where am I? There's way too much shrubbery here to be my bedroom. Hey, wait a minute. This is Mom's health spa. And who's that walking across the lobby? Let's see. Cute little dog that looks an awful lot like Maisha's pet, Truffles. A wall of security guys bigger than the Raiders' defensive line. Signature orange floppy hat . . .

Omigosh! She's here! She's here! I cannot believe it. Maisha is here! And so am I! And so is—my mother? Her face is about two inches from mine and she's asking, "Isn't that Maisha?"

Suddenly, Raven's world turned right-side up again. She was back in her bedroom, still holding the Maisha CD in her trembling hand. The plant life was gone, and her best friend was standing right in front of her.

"Chelsea," Raven said in a hushed whisper. "I just had a vision that Maisha is going to be at the same spa as my mom this weekend."

"What?" Chelsea squealed.

Raven clapped her hands together. "I can finally meet my idol!" she cried.

"Oh, gosh!" Chelsea exclaimed. The girls screamed and hugged.

Raven sighed with pure joy. "That means I'll just have to get there and ditch my mom so I can have some *real* fun with Maisha."

Raven snatched her bright orange athletic bag. She began to stuff it with things she'd need on her trip to meet her favorite pop diva of all time.

"Guess what, Missy," Chelsea said, reaching into her bag. She pulled out a blue spiral-bound notebook and opened it up. "You've got to get me her autograph, okay," she begged, thrusting the book into Raven's hand. "Have her sign right here next to my cousin's autograph." Chelsea pointed at the spot.

Raven's brow wrinkled in confusion. "Your cousin's not famous."

"Not *yet*," said Chelsea. "But we are expecting *big* things from Earl!"

Earl? Raven shook her head. Well, if Earl wants to be a recording artist, she thought, I certainly hope the first "big thing" he does is change his name!

Chapter Two

I'm hearing that spacey New Age music again, Raven thought. So I *must* be in the right place!

With her mother at her side, Raven strolled past a sign that read: QUIET PLEASE, YOGA CLASS IN PROGRESS. Together they crossed the serene, plant-filled lobby of the Silent Gardens Health Spa. From hidden speakers, quiet chimes rang.

The trouble with "meditative and restful" sounds, Raven thought, is that they put you to sleep. What this place needs is some good old-school hip-hop!

Other than the sleepy-time tunes, Raven had to admit the spa was everything her mom said it would be. The place was sleek and clean with trickling fountains and plants galore. The walls were decorated with beautiful Asian art. Dark teakwood tables held flower arrangements, delicate sculptures, and antique vases.

Raven and Mrs. Baxter strolled across the polished marble floor of the lobby and paused at an open archway where a yoga class was in session. On straw floor mats, a dozen guests in leotards followed the lead of a young instructor.

All around them, guests wrapped in beautiful gray silk robes headed for relaxing massages, restful saunas, or soothing mud baths. Raven had to admit, her mother was right. This place was amazing!

"Oh, Mom," she gushed, "this is *so fancy!*"

The yoga instructor looked up, annoyed at the sound of Raven's loud voice. A clerk at the reception desk shushed them.

Mrs. Baxter touched her finger to her lips.

"Honey," she whispered, "it's *Silent* Gardens."

My bad! Raven thought, looking around apologetically. "I'm sorry, I didn't—"

Quickly taking Raven's arm, Mrs. Baxter led her daughter to the stairs. "I'll show you around," she whispered.

Raven checked out the view through the floor-to-ceiling windows. There was a big, blue pool outside with a cascading waterfall.

"Isn't it beautiful?" Mrs. Baxter said with a sigh. "So peaceful and quiet."

"Yes," said Raven. "Definitely a place where, say, a famous pop star might hang out!" Just the idea of seeing Maisha excited Raven so much that she flung out her arms. Her bright orange athletic bag swung wide and knocked a priceless, antique vase off its stand.

Mrs. Baxter dived forward, snatching the vase out of the air before it hit the ground. "Raven!" she squealed.

Across the lobby, the receptionist shushed her. Then Raven turned and put her finger to her lips. "Shhh, Mom," she said. "It's *Silent* Gardens, remember?"

With the large vase balanced precariously in her arms, Raven's mother groaned in frustration. Then she set the vase down. "I'm going to check in," she told Raven.

"And I'll go check out this yoga class," Raven replied.

Raven hurried down to the class. She began moving from one straw mat to the next, checking the face of each guest. You never know, she told herself. One of these twisted-pretzel people just might be a certain pop diva!

"Excuse me," Raven whispered as she went from mat to mat. "Diva checking . . . diva checking . . ."

The search for Maisha was tricky because the entire yoga class had assumed odd positions. But Raven was determined to examine all the likely candidates.

Across the room, Raven spied a woman bent over her ankles. Raven crouched down on all fours until she could peer into the woman's face. It wasn't Maisha—not even close!

"Oh, sorry, sorry about that," stammered Raven. Then she spied a muscular young man. Raven moved next to him and winked.

"Hey, how ya doin'?" she said flirtatiously. "My name is Raven."

The instructor shot Raven an angry look. And she pretended to be interested in the young man's yoga pose. "How you do that? How you do that?" Raven asked.

Raven could see the instructor glaring at her. She tried to mimic the poses so she wouldn't get thrown out of the class. Unfortunately, the next pose was extreme. She had to bend all the way over and grab her ankles. Just then, from between her legs, she spied a familiar sight. It was the one, the only—Maisha!

Just like her vision, Raven saw everything upside down. The pop star was walking across the lobby. She was surrounded by big body-guards in dark suits. She had on her signature orange hat. And in her arms, she carried her fluffy little white dog, Truffles.

"There she is!" Raven gushed.

Suddenly, Mrs. Baxter's face popped into Raven's line of sight. "Isn't that Maisha?" her mother asked, wide-eyed.

Raven stood upright and brushed the hair away from her face. I can't let my mom know I had a vision of this—that Maisha is the only reason I came here, she thought.

Swallowing her excitement, Raven replied in the calmest voice she could manage. "Really? What a surprise."

As Maisha moved across the lobby, she

hugged her little dog and gave him a kiss. Then she turned to the biggest bodyguard in her entourage. "Listen, Carl," the pop star said to the giant in the dark suit. "After my yoga class, book a Swedish massage for me and a seaweed wrap for my Truffles."

The man nodded his shaved head and wrote down the instructions on a notepad. Once again, Maisha nuzzled her pampered pet. Truffles happily licked the diva's cheek.

"Oh, and listen," added Maisha. "Make *sure* we're not disturbed."

Carl nodded, tucked the notebook into his jacket, then glanced suspiciously at the guests in the lobby.

Mrs. Baxter turned to Raven. "Too bad we didn't bring a camera," she said.

Raven could hardly contain her glee. "I'm *sure* I can dig one up," she said coolly. Like right out of my bag, she joked to herself. Then she reached in, dug around, and pulled out one of the *three* disposable cameras she'd packed that morning!

"This is just too easy," Raven whispered to herself with a sly grin.

But before Raven could take her first picture, Mrs. Baxter was already heading for the pop star. *Omigosh*, thought Raven in a panic, what is my mom doing?!

"Oh, what a cute little doggie," Mrs. Baxter squealed, walking right up to Truffles and Maisha.

"Code Red! Swarm! Swarm!" Carl shouted as he flung himself between Maisha and Mrs. Baxter. Before Raven's mom knew what hit her, Carl and another bodyguard had lifted her by her elbows and moved her out of Maisha's way. The other guards formed a wall of flesh around the diva and hustled her up the stairs and out of sight.

"I *just* wanted to pet the dog," Mrs. Baxter protested.

Carl the bodyguard loomed over Mrs. Baxter. "Not on my watch, ma'am," he told her in a stern voice.

Raven nervously shoved the camera back into her bag. She felt the bodyguard's cold blue eyes watching her. Shifting uncomfortably, Raven offered Carl an innocent smile, then hurried away.

"This could be a little tougher than I thought," whispered Raven.

She was still determined to meet her favorite pop star, of course. She just had to come up with a plan that didn't include getting "swarmed" by a posse of creepy linebackers in dark suits.

Chapter Three

Meanwhile, back at the Baxter house, Raven's dad was happily humming as he cooked. He wore a colorful apron and a white chef's hat on his head. He also wore a big smile as he carried an armful of dinner plates, forks, knives, and spoons out of the kitchen and into the living room.

Mr. Baxter laid out three place settings on the coffee table, then announced, "Okay, gang! While Mrs. B and Raven are at the spa getting their *rub* on, we're gonna get our *grub* on!"

Cory, Chelsea, and Eddie gathered around the coffee table and grinned expectantly.

"Did you hook us up with something special, Mr. B?" Eddie asked.

Mr. Baxter shook his head. "No. I've got a new dish I want you to try. I'm going to add it to The Chill Grill menu."

Raven's brother, Cory, stood up and grabbed the waistband of his oversized sweatpants. "I hope it's your blueberry cobbler, Dad," he declared, "'cause I got my eatin' pants on." Cory released the elastic. *Snap!* went the waistband.

Mr. Baxter shook his head. "No, it's not the cobbler. It's even better. It's my mother's famous pickled artichoke mashed potatoes." He turned to Raven's best friend. "Eddie, remember? I made 'em for the block party last year?"

Eddie remembered all right. And, for the briefest moment, his expression was paralyzed in horror. But he didn't want to hurt Mr. Baxter's feelings, so he quickly forced a grin.

"Man, those spuds were off the chart, Mr. B," he lied.

Chelsea had also hated that vile dish. But she was not going to be the one to tell Mr. Baxter the truth. If Eddie was going to lie, then so was she. "Yeah," she said, smiling stiffly, "I *love* that stuff."

"Well, great," Mr. Baxter replied. "'Cause I made a *huge* pot."

Mr. Baxter turned and went back to the kitchen. As soon as he was out of earshot, Chelsea's smile turned upside down. "Okay, I *hate* that stuff," she whispered to Eddie and Cory.

Eddie frowned. "I don't get it. Mr. B's a great cook, but that dish is pure evil."

Chelsea shuddered. "Well, what are we going to do?" she asked. "We can't tell him. It's his mother's treasured recipe. We'll just hurt his feelings."

Cory sighed and shook his head. "He's *my* dad. I should be the one to tell him."

Eddie and Chelsea nodded, impressed by Cory's sudden maturity. Just then, the kitchen doors swung wide open. Mr. Baxter excitedly strode into the room. He was carrying a massive silver pot of sea-green mashed potatoes.

"Okay," said Mr. Baxter, lifting a large wooden spoon. "Who's ready?"

"They are!" Cory cried. Without hesitation, he pointed to Eddie and Chelsea.

Chelsea's jaw dropped, and Eddie narrowed his eyes on the little stinker. Excuse you, Eddie thought. What happened to *I should be the one to tell him!*

Splat! . . . *Splat!* Mr. Baxter slapped oozing green globs onto Chelsea's and Eddie's plates. Cory could hardly contain his laughter at their stricken expressions—until his father got around to loading up Cory's plate with the stuff, too.

"Mmm, yummy." Chelsea had to force the

words out of her mouth. "Pickled artichokes and potatoes. It's a marriage made in heaven." She waved her hand, trying to disperse the stink rising to her nostrils. She could hardly stand the smell.

Mr. Baxter smiled down at Eddie. "Hey, my man," he said. "I remember at the block party your plate disappeared like that. So I am giving you a *double* helping!" With that, Mr. Baxter plopped yet another slimy mound of green gunk onto the first one.

With dread, Eddie gazed down at the sea of green. "Man, Mr. B," said Eddie. "This is really going to hit the spot . . . and *stay* there." At least I hope it stays there, Eddie thought. He swallowed hard, trying not to gag and hurl right in front of the chef.

Beaming happily, Mr. Baxter presented Cory with the long wooden spoon. It was caked with greenish sludge. "And, son," he said proudly, "you get to lick the spoon."

Cory took the spoon and held it at arm's length. "Uh . . . th-thanks, Dad," he stammered.

Mr. Baxter stared at Cory. He couldn't wait to see his son's expression when he took that first bite!

Cory gulped. He closed his eyes. Finally, he took a lick. "Mmmmm," he moaned. But he was really thinking, *Blech!* This stuff is even more gross than I remember!

But even Cory didn't have the heart to burst his dad's chef bubble. Forcing a thumbs-up, he said, "Kapowee!"

Still beaming, Mr. Baxter turned to Eddie and Chelsea. "Go ahead, guys, dig in!" he cried.

"Oh, all right," Eddie replied, trying to sound enthusiastic. "That's all you had to say, Mr. B."

Mr. Baxter watched proudly as Eddie and Chelsea took their first mouthfuls. They both made "oohhhs" and "aahhhs," and Mr. Baxter nodded his head.

"I'm going to go start on a *second* batch," he declared.

As soon as Mr. B was gone, Eddie and Chelsea opened their mouths and spit the green spuds back onto their plates. Cory guzzled water to kill the taste.

Eddie glared at Cory. "What happened, *dawg*?" he cried. "I thought you were going to say something."

"I couldn't," Cory replied. "He looked so happy."

"Well, c'mon," Chelsea said. "We have to get rid of this first batch before he comes out with a second batch."

Cory looked around for a good spud-dumping location. The couch cushions? The potted plant? The back of the television? "But where can we stash it?" he asked.

Eddie and Chelsea shared a look, then faced Cory. "Pants!" they cried, pointing to his elastic waistband.

Cory stared at Raven's friends for a few seconds before he realized, *yes*, they were perfectly serious!

"Oh, man," Cory said with a groan.

But he didn't have a better idea. Plus, Eddie and Chelsea were bigger and stronger—and they outnumbered him. Reluctantly, Cory stretched out his waistband and grimaced.

Chelsea and Eddie wasted no time. With their forks and spoons, they quickly scraped the green goo off their plates—and down Cory's pants.

Chapter Four

Raven paced the spa's hallways wearing her pink-and-white workout clothes. On her shoulder hung her bright orange athletic bag. Inside were the three cameras and Chelsea's autograph book.

I am *going* to get to Maisha, she told herself. It's only a matter of time!

After twenty minutes of hanging around the halls, Raven finally saw Carl the bodyguard. Her pulse raced. Wherever that creepy bodyguard went, her favorite pop diva was sure to follow!

When Raven saw Carl heading for the yoga room, she thought fast. There was a second entrance to the room, so she slipped through it. She ducked behind a Japanese silk screen and crouched next to a table holding a pair of finger cymbals and a vase of flowers.

Raven peeked around the screen to see Carl touching his hand to the headset in his ear. "All clear," he transmitted to another bodyguard. "Bring in Maisha for her private yoga session."

Maisha entered the room wearing a white warm-up suit and matching jacket. Three of her dark-suited security detail followed. Little Truffles sat inside a bright orange athletic bag hanging from Maisha's shoulder.

Carl put a hand to his headset again. "Right," he said, "I copy that." Then the bodyguard frowned and faced the pop star. "Bad news, Maisha. Your yoga instructor is stuck in traffic, she's going to be a little late."

Raven's eyes widened as an idea struck her. She picked up the finger cymbals sitting on the table. Then she pulled a swath of silky fabric down off the Japanese screen.

Oh, yeah, this is going to work, Raven told herself. She wrapped the fabric around her waist to make it look like an exotic sarong. Then she slipped the cymbals onto her thumb and index finger.

On the other side of the screen, Maisha was trying to cope with the bad news about her yoga instructor. "Okay," she said, "I'm here to relax." But in the middle of her deep, calming breath, the diva stomped her foot. "So, I'm *not* going to let it bother me that the whole world is incompetent!"

Whoa, Raven thought, my girl is totally stressing. Time for Relaxing Raven to make her entrance. She glided forward and struck her tiny brass finger cymbals. *Ching!*

Maisha and her bodyguards looked up to see Raven emerging from behind the silk screen.

"Hello," said Raven in a soft, breathy voice. "I am the yoga teacher." She touched her little cymbals together again. *Ching!* "I was stuck in traffic, but now . . . I'm unstuck." *Ching!*

Raven glided up to Carl the giant. "So if I could just get to Maisha to start my private yoga class—" She waited for Carl to step aside, but he refused to move a muscle. Then she tried to step around him, and he blocked her path with a warning glare.

"—or you could just join the class," Raven added nervously.

"You know what?" Maisha demanded impatiently. "Could we just get started? 'Cause I'm a bundle of nerves."

"Oh, then we should definitely unbundle those nerves," cooed Raven, touching the cymbals together again. *Ching!*

Carl laid out a mat for Maisha, and a smaller, matching mat for Truffles. The fluffy white dog jumped out of the orange bag and onto the small mat. Maisha positioned herself on the large mat and stared at Raven.

For a second Raven just stared back. She could not believe she was in the same room with her idol! She wanted to scream and shout and jump up and down. But the thought of Carl doing his "swarm" thing on her brought her back to earth.

Okay, now what? Raven asked herself. Maisha is expecting private yoga instruction. *Dang,* what do I do first? . . . Oh, I know!

Standing tall and confident, Raven softly announced, "Let's get started with something I like to call—" *Ching!* "—breathing."

Raven flung her arms wide. "Breathing," she said. "Breathing, okay, we're going to start with some simple breathing. . . . Breathe in. . . ."

Raven and Maisha both took deep breaths. As Raven held hers, she nervously watched

Carl. He was still hovering on the sidelines, keeping a suspicious eye on her.

"And breathe out—" Raven gasped. "Breathe in. . . . Breathe out. . . . Fabulous!" Raven said. As she led the breathing exercise, she slowly moved closer to Maisha.

Out of the corner of her eye, she noticed Carl frowning in her direction. Their eyes met and Carl stepped closer—so close that Raven had to step back.

"I'm starting to feel some bad vibes," Raven complained to Maisha. "*And* some bad breath." She narrowed her eyes at Carl.

"You know what?" snapped the pop diva. "Maisha is *bored* with breathing."

"And that ends the breathing portion of our program!" Raven quickly declared.

Maisha tapped her foot impatiently. "So when are we going to get to the *poses*?" she asked.

"Right," said Raven, stalling for time. "To the poses." *Ching!* "The first thing we're going to pose as is—"

Raven desperately searched the room for a clue. *Dang*, she thought, isn't there a Yoga Pose of the Month calendar on the wall? Finally, Raven's eyes fell on a small clay statue of—

"—a turtle," she told Maisha.

The diva blinked in surprise. "A turtle? I've never heard of that pose."

"That's because it's *new*," Raven quickly replied.

Maisha shrugged. "All right, let's get started."

Raven raised her arms over her head, then tucked them close to her body. "Bring your arms in, everyone," she announced. Maisha moved along with her, but the bodyguards just stared. "I said *everyone* in the room," Raven snapped. "Arms in like you're grabbing the air. Legs around, circular motion, arch the back!"

Maisha glared at her bodyguards. They quickly copied Raven's movements. The only one not doing the "new" turtle pose was Truffles, who was too busy sniffing a table leg.

"Down! Head down!" Raven ordered like a drill sergeant, until everyone's head was down, their chins touching their chests. "Now bring your head into your hands and close your eyes." When everyone's face was covered, Raven smiled. "Fabulous. Now I would like all of the *boy* turtles to step to the back of the room. . . ."

Hunched over in a turtle pose, hands over his face, Carl rolled his eyes. But like the other bodyguards, he obeyed and scuttled to the back.

"Fabulous," cooed Raven. "All right now . . ."

As soon as the bodyguards were far enough away, Raven grabbed her orange athletic bag from under the table. Then she tiptoed over to

Maisha and tapped her gently. "Maisha . . ." Raven whispered.

"Am I a good turtle?" Maisha asked.

"Yes," said Raven. "Yes, you are. You're the best turtle I've ever seen, yeah!"

Finally, Raven dropped her masquerade. "Maisha, I just want you to know, I'm your biggest fan. And if you wouldn't mind hookin' a sister up with a picture and a few auto-graphs?"

Raven reached into her athletic bag. She pulled out one of her disposable cameras and Chelsea's autograph book. Then she dropped the bag again. Truffles trotted over and began to sniff it.

"Here. Sign right here, next to Earl," said Raven, thrusting a pen into Maisha's hand.

Maisha's serene yoga face twisted into an outraged grimace. "What is this?!" she cried.

Carl looked up from his turtle pose. And

Raven panicked. "Carl, back in your shell!" she commanded. "Right now! *Zen!*" Then Raven lifted her camera and aimed it at the pop diva. "It's nothing, girl, just smile big for the camera."

The flashbulb went off in Maisha's face, temporarily blinding the diva. "What are you doing?!" she screeched. "I have sensitive retinas. Will you get her out of here?!"

Startled by the commotion, Truffles found a place to hide—inside Raven's athletic bag! As the bodyguards swarmed to grab Raven, she snatched up her bag. "No, stop, bad turtles!" she cried. But the bodyguards just kept coming.

Okay, girl, think fast, Raven told herself. She pointed to the door. "Look!" she shouted at the muscle-bound crew. "Free protein shakes!"

All the bodyguards stopped and looked.

Psych! Raven thought as she slung her athletic bag over her shoulder and took off running.

After she was gone, Maisha realized her little dog was nowhere in sight. "Truffles, Truffles! Are you okay?" Maisha cried.

The bodyguards looked around the room, but Maisha's beloved Truffles was gone. Maisha was frantic. She screamed and clutched her head. "That girl dognapped my baby! Get her! I want her arrested!"

The bodyguards took off running, hot on Raven's heels.

Chapter Five

Raven raced through the busy lobby to a hallway leading to the massage-therapy rooms. She paused and peeked over her shoulder. There was no sign of Carl or the other burly bodyguards.

Phew! Raven thought. "Glad that's over!"

But it wasn't. A few seconds later, she heard the thunder of heavy footsteps. Carl swung around the corner and met Raven's wide-eyed stare.

"There she is!" he bellowed. "Swarm! Swarm!"

Raven spun and ran in the opposite direction. She still had no idea that little Truffles was inside her bag! Rounding another corner, she noticed an open door. She ran inside and quickly closed it behind her. Holding her breath, she listened to the footsteps of the bodyguards running down the hall, right past the room she was in.

Outfoxed you again, Carl! she thought.

Suddenly, Raven heard loud breathing behind her. She wasn't alone! Spinning around, she saw her mother sitting on a massage table, wearing one of those gray silk Silent Gardens robes.

Mrs. Baxter didn't notice her daughter right away. She was too busy reciting a soothing mantra and practicing deep breathing exercises. "Se-re-ni-ty," she chanted through a tranquil smile.

Ah, yes, thought Mrs. Baxter, her eyes closed. This is the reason I'm here. Quiet. Peace. Tranquillity at last.

"Mom! Big problem," Raven cried, rushing up to the table.

Mrs. Baxter's eyes snapped open. "Serenity *over*," she said with a sigh.

Raven tugged on Mrs. Baxter's robe. "Mom, you won't believe what's going on!"

"Oh, I heard," Mrs. Baxter replied, climbing down off the table. "Somebody stole Maisha's dog, and now she wants to have the woman arrested."

Raven gasped. "What?" She hadn't heard all that about the dog. "Well, I don't blame her," she told her mother. "What kind of a creep would steal poor little old Truffles?" For some reason, Raven's athletic bag felt heavier than usual. She set it on the table.

Ruff! Ruff! Ruff!

Raven's eyes went wide as Truffles poked his cute little head out of her orange bag. "Oh, snap! *I'm* the creep," she cried in horror.

Mrs. Baxter's jaw dropped. "Raven, you stole the dog!"

Raven shook her head. "No. He must have jumped into my bag when I was pretending to be Maisha's yoga teacher."

"What?" Mrs. Baxter stared at her daughter, waiting for an explanation. But she would have to wait a little longer. A loud knock interrupted them.

"Is anyone in there?" yelled Carl the bodyguard, outside the door. "We're doing a search of the area."

Mrs. Baxter jumped around in a panic. "Just a minute!" she cried. Then she grabbed Raven's arm and spoke in a loud whisper. "Rae, just give 'em back the dog and explain what happened."

Raven shook her head fearfully. "Mom, you remember when you tried to pet Truffles. These people swarm first and ask questions later."

Mrs. Baxter frowned, knowing Raven was right. But what could they possibly do? They were both trapped in here, with Carl blocking the only exit.

Another loud knock was followed by the thunder of stamping feet. Raven realized that the rest of Maisha's goon squad was now on the other side of the door.

"Ma'am, we need to come in," roared Carl in a commanding voice. "It's an emergency situation."

Out of options, Mrs. Baxter opened her oversized robe and Raven slipped inside. Quickly, Raven shoved one arm through the right side of the robe and pulled one foot beneath her on the table. Then she crouched down low, and Mrs. Baxter closed her robe again.

"Come in!" Mrs. Baxter finally cried.

The door flew open and Carl strode into the therapy room. He walked up to the massage therapy table, which held the widest woman he'd ever seen.

Carl didn't realize that Raven's arm was sticking out of the robe's right sleeve. And her mother's arm was sticking out of the left. Beneath the closed robe, dangled two legs. One was Raven's with a pink shoe. And the other was her mother's with a white shoe.

"Ma'am, have you seen a yoga-teaching, celebrity pooch-napper?" Carl asked.

Mrs. Baxter met the bodyguard's suspicious stare with one of her own. "Excuse *me*," she said in a wounded tone, "can't a large woman relax in peace? Just because my head is dispro-portional to my body doesn't mean I don't deserve my privacy!"

"Right. Sorry," said Carl. Mrs. Baxter's tone had done the trick. He actually looked guilty. But before he turned to go, he said, "A word of warning. This girl's dangerous, so if you see her, call me. Because I'm taking her down."

Carl reached into his jacket and produced a

business card. He offered it to Mrs. Baxter. Unfortunately, he was standing on Raven's side of the robe. Blindly, Raven's arm groped for the card. Finally, Mrs. Baxter just slapped her daughter's hand aside and grabbed the card with her own hand.

Carl was nearly out the door when Truffles peeked out from under the huge robe and growled. The bodyguard whirled, but he was too late. Mrs. Baxter had already pushed Truffles back under her robe again.

"Oh, that's my stomach growling," Mrs. Baxter lied as she patted her tummy. "Uh, hush, stomach. Stay, stomach. Stay! Good stomach. Good stomach."

Carl gazed at Mrs. Baxter for a final moment. Then the man left. Mrs. Baxter immediately opened her robe. Raven rolled out, gasping for air and clutching Truffles to her heart.

Mrs. Baxter caught her daughter's arm. "Okay, Raven," she said, nearly out of patience. "Do you want to tell me what's going on?"

"Well . . . the *real* reason I came to the spa with you," she confessed, "was because I had a vision that Maisha was here and I wanted to meet her."

Mrs. Baxter's frowned. "So you lied. You didn't come here to have fun with me," she said. Raven could see the hurt and disappointment in her mother's eyes.

"This is fun," Raven said weakly.

Mrs. Baxter just crossed her arms and glared.

Meanwhile, in the Baxters' living room, Eddie was having about as much "fun" as Raven. Mr. Baxter had just slapped another giant glob of green potatoes onto his plate, and Eddie felt his stomach lurch.

Man, he thought, the pickled stench of artichokes is really messing me up.

"You cleaned your plates. Time to dirty 'em up again!" Mr. Baxter said with a laugh as he dished up big servings for Chelsea and Cory, too.

Chelsea reared back when the potatoes hit her plate. Cory didn't and was splashed by the mess. *Begone*, you evil potatoes, he thought. But not even a curse could get rid of the vile pile.

"Okay, guys, look, I've got to take a shower and get ready for work," said Mr. Baxter. He set the pot of spuds at Eddie's elbow. "I'm going to leave this for you right here."

Everyone looked up at Mr. Baxter with blank stares. "C'mon, dig in!" cried Raven's dad. He waited until everyone had a mouthful before he finally turned and headed upstairs. When Mr. Baxter was out of sight, all three spit the potatoes onto their plates.

"*Ugh*, this is awful," Chelsea said, gagging.

Eddie grabbed the pot and waved Cory forward. "Come here."

"No way!" Cory cried, grabbing his waistband. "No more potatoes in my pants."

Chelsea noticed how the pants had expanded, and patted the bulging material. "They make a squishy sound," she observed.

Cory ran behind the couch, and Chelsea set down her plate. "You know what?" she said. "Cory's right. His tank is full. Let's dump this in the sink."

"The sink!" Eddie exclaimed with a grin. "Chels, you're such a genius."

Chelsea blinked blankly. "Really? 'Cause I don't actually get that a lot."

"Can we move this along?" Cory shifted uncomfortably. "This first batch is starting to harden!"

Eddie grabbed the pot, Chelsea collected

the plates, and they hurried into the kitchen. Cory waddled after them.

In the kitchen, Eddie, Chelsea, and Cory learned something new. Dumping potatoes into the *sink* doesn't mean you can actually get them down the *drain*.

Chelsea ran water, and Eddie pushed the greenish mess around with a spoon. But the goo just kept on bubbling up out of the drain like a living thing.

"It's not going down!" Cory said fearfully.

"Man! The sink won't swallow this stuff either!" Eddie cried.

They all grabbed spoons and pummeled the green sludge before it overflowed the sink. The blob bubbled and churned. Finally, the drain made a loud sucking sound followed by a gurgling. The sludge went down, down, down until the gurgling ended with a final burp.

"It's gone," said Eddie, clearly relieved.

"We saved ourselves," Cory declared.

Chelsea nodded. "More importantly, we saved mankind."

Cory moved to the kitchen table and sat down. His pants made a squishy sound, and he grimaced.

Suddenly, the kitchen door burst open and Mr. Baxter charged in. He was wearing a damp bathrobe. Under it, he was soaking wet and covered from head to toe in a greenish sludge.

"Oh, man. I've got to call a plumber," Mr. Baxter said, reaching for the phone. "There's a weird slime coming out of the shower."

Some of the green muck slid down his cheek. He sniffed it. "Why does this slime smell like Grandma's potatoes?" Mr. B asked.

Eddie and Chelsea traded a guilty look. Then Eddie sighed. "Well, uh, 'cause we kind of dumped them down the sink and they kind of backed up through the shower?" he said sheepishly.

Mr. Baxter scratched his head. "Why did you dump them down the sink?" he asked.

Chelsea shrugged. Isn't it obvious? she thought. "'Cause Cory's pants were full."

Now Mr. Baxter was really confused. "Full of *what*?" he asked.

"Your potatoes," Cory said, waddling up to his father. "Dad, they're just *nasty*."

Mr. Baxter frowned. "Why didn't you tell me that you didn't like them?"

"We didn't want to hurt your feelings," Eddie confessed.

To everyone's surprise, Mr. Baxter began to laugh. "Well," he admitted, "to tell you the truth, I never liked them, either!"

Cory's eyebrows rose. "So, why do you keep making them?"

"Well, you told me you liked them," his

father replied. Then the lightbulb went off as he realized—"That is exactly what I used to tell *my* mom."

Mr. Baxter shook his head. "Okay, guys, from now on if you don't like something, just tell me. Okay?"

Eddie grinned, relieved. "Cool with me."

Chelsea quickly agreed. "Yeah, cool."

Cory took a deep breath. "Well, Dad, I've got to tell you—since we're being honest. Your *potatoes* are rubbing me the wrong way."

Mr. Baxter waved his hand. "Cory, I already *know* you don't like them."

But Cory shook his head and grabbed the waistband of his bulging pants. "No, they are *rubbing* me the wrong way! I've got to get out of these pants!"

Then Mr. Baxter, Eddie, and Chelsea all watched Cory waddle toward the stairs to change into something less . . . potato-ish.

Chapter Six

Back at the Silent Gardens Health Spa, Raven hid inside the massage-therapy room. Maisha's dog, Truffles, sat inside the athletic bag hanging on Raven's shoulder.

Suddenly, the door opened and Mrs. Baxter hurried inside. She closed the door behind her. "Okay," she told Raven. "I found out that Maisha's massage is in here in five minutes. So we leave the dog. Maisha finds him. We hit the road, and we'll pretend like this never happened."

Raven nodded enthusiastically. "Oh, man, I love that plan. Especially the *pretending* part."

Raven placed the bag on the table and opened it. Out jumped Truffles. "Come here,

Truffles," said Raven, taking the dog. "Auntie Raven's going to leave you here to find your mommy." Then Raven waved a warning finger under the pooch's cold, wet, button nose.

"Don't go into any more strange bags," Raven advised the dog. "Not good."

With Truffles waiting on the massage table, Raven and Mrs. Baxter headed for the door. But they both froze when they heard a familiar voice on the other side of it. Maisha was already here! She was talking to Carl and the rest of her bodyguards!

"I'm going to be in here getting my massage," she told them.

Raven was frantic. "Why is she early?" she whispered to her mom. "I thought divas were always *late*!"

"And listen," Maisha loudly continued on the other side of the door. "You better guard the door 'cause I heard that maniac is still on the loose."

Raven stuffed Truffles back into her athletic bag. Then she and Mrs. Baxter scrambled around, looking in vain for a place to hide. Finally they dived under the massage table, which was covered by a long, white sheet.

A moment later, the door slid open and the pop star entered the room wearing one of the spa's gray silk robes. She leaned against the massage table and rubbed her forehead.

"I really need this massage," Maisha muttered. "This has been the worst day of my life. And I miss my Truffles."

With a sigh, Maisha closed her eyes and stretched out, belly down, across the massage table. She carefully lowered her face into the oval opening at the end of the table. When she opened her eyes again, the pop star saw Mrs. Baxter looking up at her from beneath the table.

"Who are you?" Maisha screamed.

Mrs. Baxter stammered for a moment, then replied in her best fake Swedish accent. "*Gutentag*, hello, *und* vat's up-in?" said Mrs. Baxter. "I'm Inga, your Svedish *masseuse*."

"What are you doing under the table?" Maisha demanded, her face still peering through the hole in the table.

Mrs. Baxter gulped. "This is vhere vee start!" she replied. Then she reached up, grabbed Maisha's lips, and started twisting them. "Ve start vith zee lips. Ve pull and ve pull like milking da cow."

Maisha shook Mrs. Baxter's hands off her face. "My lips are fine," she said. "All the tension is in my neck."

Mrs. Baxter looked at Raven, who was under the table, too, but well out of sight.

Go, Mom, Raven said, silently mouthing the words. Mrs. Baxter shrugged and rolled out from under the table. She stood up and immediately began massaging Maisha's back.

"Here ve go," said Mrs. Baxter. "Kneadin' da necken', like a Svedish meatball."

"Wait a minute! What are you doing?" snapped Maisha. "Where's the *oil*?"

Mrs. Baxter realized her mistake.

"Ya, da oil. Where is the oil?" said Mrs. Baxter.

She frantically looked around for massage oil. A plastic bottle sat on a table across the room, right next to an enormous jug of the stuff. She leaned down and waved for Raven to fetch it.

"Got to get da oil," she babbled. "For massagin' the neckin'. Here we going . . . just a moment on the oil!"

Raven rolled out from under the massage table. She grabbed the squeeze bottle and handed it to her mom. Mrs. Baxter tried to pour some oil into her hand, but the bottle was empty!

From the massage table, Maisha cried out impatiently. "Everyone, what's taking so long?" In frustration, she began to lift her head out of the hole in the table. Mrs. Baxter pushed her back down.

"So much tension in da neck," said Mrs. Baxter, hastily kneading the woman's muscles. "Got to relax and let it go!"

Raven snatched the empty bottle back from her mother and hurried to refill it from the massive jug. Gripping the bottle between her knees, Raven lifted the heavy jug, then tipped it over. Massage oil gushed out of the spout. Some of the oil ended up in the plastic bottle, but most of it spilled onto the floor. Soon the whole area was covered in a thin sheen of slimy massage oil.

Finally, the bottle became so slippery that it

shot out from between Raven's knees. Mrs. Baxter lunged and snatched it out of the air.

Score, she thought. Looks like all that Frisbee playing in college paid off! "Gotten de oil!" she cried.

Suddenly, Truffles hopped out of Raven's athletic bag and tried to trot across the slippery floor. As Mrs. Baxter and Raven watched in horror, the little dog sniffed Maisha's hand as it dangled over the edge of the massage table.

Panicked, Mrs. Baxter signaled for Raven to catch the dog. Raven took a single step—then hit the floor when her feet touched the oil. She landed with a slap in the grease.

Scrambling onto her hands and knees, Raven crawled across the oil-soaked floor. She grabbed the little dog just as Maisha lifted her head from the table—and came face-to-face with Raven and Truffles.

Raven gave Maisha an uneasy grin. "How y'all doin'?"

"It's *you*," the diva screamed. "And you've got my Truffles!"

Raven opened her mouth to explain but before she could get one word out, Maisha was bellowing, "Caaaaaaarl!"

The door instantly opened, and the big man appeared. His eyes met Raven's, and a grin stretched across his face. "Oh, I've got ya now, missy," he growled.

Carl lunged forward to grab Raven. But when his feet hit the oil, he slid across the room and into a pile of towels.

Truffles began barking and Maisha called, "Truffles! Come to mama!"

The dog took off in a run for its mom. But its little furry paws slipped across the slick floor and Truffles slid right out the door!

"Truffles! No!" screamed Raven. She tried

to run after the dog, but slipped instead. She landed on her rump and slid into the hall, too, right behind Truffles!

"Don't you touch my baby!" Maisha cried out as she jumped off the massage table. Immediately, the pop star slid out the door— right behind Tuffles and Raven!

"I'll get her, ma'am," yelled Carl.

Knocking a teakwood table aside, Carl stumbled to his feet and fell right back down again. Squirming helplessly, the huge body-guard slid across the oil-slick floor like a penguin on ice—right behind Truffles, Raven, and Maisha!

When Mrs. Baxter saw the big man chasing her daughter, she lunged forward. "Don't you touch *my* baby!" she cried. Then *she* took a turn slipping across the floor and out the door—right behind Truffles, Raven, Maisha, and Carl the bodyguard!

Everyone ended up in a twisted heap. Maisha struggled to get to her feet but was trapped by Carl, who lay sprawled across her.

"Get off of me, Bigfoot!" the diva yelled.

Raven sat up, lifted little Truffles out of the mess, and handed the dog to Maisha. "I believe this belongs to you."

Maisha took Truffles and held the little dog close. Truffles licked her face and wagged his fluffly white tail while Maisha cooed. "Oh, Truffles. Oh, baby. Mommy was so worried about you. Did the bad little girl hurt you?"

"No," said Raven. "That was an accident."

But Maisha wouldn't hear it. "Carl!" she cried, pointing to Raven. "Don't just stand there. Get her *out* of here."

Mrs. Baxter leaped to her feet and jumped between the bodyguard and her daughter. "Back off, Carl!" Mrs. Baxter warned.

"Wait a minute," Maisha said. "How can

you stand there and defend this, this sick, twisted little—"

Mrs. Baxter stuck her finger in the pop star's face. "Hold on, girlfriend," she barked. "I know you're a pop diva, but *nobody* talks that way about my daughter."

Maisha threw back her head. "Well, *your* daughter stole *my* Truffles," she shot back.

Mrs. Baxter lowered her finger, and her voice. "Look, Maisha," she said. "My daughter Raven is your biggest fan. All she wanted to do was meet you."

Raven stepped forward. "Yeah, Maisha. And get a couple of autographs, a couple of pictures, maybe a lock of hair."

Mrs. Baxter shot Raven an angry look. Hands on hips, she addressed her daughter. "Raven, I think someone owes somebody an apology."

Raven nodded in agreement. She turned

to face Bigfoot. "And Carl, I accept," she said.

"*Raven!*" scolded Mrs. Baxter.

Raven sighed and stepped up to the pop star. "Maisha, I'm sorry I ruined your weekend," she said sincerely. Then Raven faced her mother. "Mom, I'm sorry I lied to you just so I could meet Maisha."

Maisha blinked at Raven's words. "So that's it, huh? You lied to your *own* mother just to meet *me*?"

Raven nodded, ashamed. But Maisha thought it was the coolest thing she'd ever heard. "Oh girl, so cool and so sweet!" she told Raven. "You *go*, girl!" Then she turned to her bodyguard and snapped her fingers. "Carl, don't just stand there, get me one of my CDs and a pen. Because Maisha's got some autographs to sign!"

Rolling his eyes, Carl did as he was told. As Maisha signed her recording, Raven faced her mother. "You know, Mom, despite everything that's happened today, I had real fun hanging out with you."

Mrs. Baxter couldn't believe her ears. "Really?" she said. "'Cause I do *a lot* of fun things. You should come to my gardening club. It's radish week!"

Raven nervously cleared her throat. "Ooh . . . that could be fun," she said. And I guess I deserve that for the way I treated you, she thought, still feeling guilty.

"*Or*," her mother added, putting her arm around Raven's shoulders, "we could go to a Maisha concert."

"Ooohh!" Raven cried excitedly.

Maisha heard their conversation and snapped her fingers again. "Carl, come up with some tickets."

"Yeah, Carl," said Raven with a grin. "Some tickets and some backstage passes, a limo ride, and, girl," she teased Maisha, "maybe you can put me on stage and I could be one of your backup dancers?" Then she began to sing, *"I'm just a simple girl with a private jet . . ."*

After all the craziness was over, Maisha invited Raven and Mrs. Baxter to spend the day with her. They met in the massage-therapy room, where an impromptu sing-along took place.

In matching robes, and towels wrapped around their heads like turbans, the girls launched into a rendition of Maisha's latest hit, using plastic squeeze bottles as if they were microphones.

Carl stood guard in the corner with Truffles resting in his arms. The little dog wore a matching silk robe, and a towel on his tiny head, too.

"I'm just a simple girl with a private jet . . ." sang Raven and Mrs. Baxter with the famous

Maisha. *"I have so much money, my friends are all in debt. I've got a lot of diamonds on my hands and feet, but I'm still Maisha from up the street!"*

"She's still Maisha!" bellowed Mrs. Baxter so loudly that Raven and Maisha stopped and stared.

"Isn't that how it goes?" Raven's mom asked sheepishly.

Maisha burst out laughing, and they all started singing again. Everyone, that is, but Carl. He just stood in the corner, shaking his head as he spoke to the dog.

"I *do not* get paid enough for this," he said with a sigh.

Gaze into the future and take a sneak peek at the next *That's So Raven* story. . . .

Adapted by Alice Alfonsi

Based on the television series, "That's So Raven", created by Michael Poryes and Susan Sherman

Based on the episode written by Beth Seriff & Geoff Tarson

"It's on!" called Raven's father from the living room.

"It's on!" echoed Raven's brother from the staircase.

In her attic bedroom, Raven Baxter heard

her family's shouts and nearly dropped her cell phone. "Got to go," she told her best friend, Chelsea Daniels. "It's on!"

Seconds later, Raven was flying down the stairs and running into the living room. Mrs. Baxter came rushing in from the kitchen, and together the whole family crowded onto the living room sofa.

Undercover Superstar was about to start!

As far as Raven and her family were concerned, *Undercover Superstar* was *the* most slammin' television show on prime time. Not only did the Baxters never miss an episode, they knew every word of its theme song by heart.

"From the East coast to the West," the family sang with the TV, *"we're lookin', we're lookin' . . . we're lookin' for the best . . . we're lookin', we're lookin' . . ."*

"Can you sing?" chirped the show's performers.

"Yeah!" cried Raven, leaping up from the couch.

"Can you dance?" asked the show's announcer.

"Yeah!" cried Raven's brother, Cory, gettin' jiggy with it.

"Lookin' for that one big chance?" asked the TV.

"Yeah, yeah, yeah, yeah . . ." cried Mr. and Mrs. Baxter, bustin' some moves of their own.

"Undercover Superstar, *we will find you wherever you are,"* promised the TV. "Undercover Superstar . . ."

"Oh, yeah, yeah," Raven sang along.

When the show's dancers threw off their trench coats and sunglasses to reveal flashy stage costumes, Raven landed on one knee. She threw out her hands and started singing the last yeahs of the theme song like a pop diva belting out an encore.

"Yee-aay, yee-aaaay, yee-aayyy-ee-aiiii-aah-ee-aiiiy!" she crooned.

In the dead silence that followed, Raven noticed her entire family frowning down at her.

Excuse *you*, she thought. . . .

"Hi, and welcome to *Undercover Superstar*," the beautiful television hostess announced, "the show where we go to your school, under-cover, to find America's next superstar. Now if you're out there, we'll find you."

The music began to play again and the show cut to commercial. As the Baxters settled back against the couch cushions, Raven crossed her legs and sighed. "Ooh, it would be so cool to be a pop star."

Mrs. Baxter grinned and slapped her daughter's knee. "You know what, honey," she said, "back in the day, your father and I came pretty close."

"Tanya!" cried Mr. Baxter, grabbing his

wife's arm. "Not in front of the children."

"C'mon, Victor," said Raven's mother, pulling her arm loose. "I think they're old enough to know about Toast and Jelly."

"Uh-oh." Raven cringed, already guessing what was coming next. "I think the question is, do we want to know about Toast and Jelly?"

"Your father was Toast," explained Mrs. Baxter, "and I was Jelly."

Oh snap, thought Raven, another trip down memory lane.

"We were on a show called *Soul Search*," Raven's mother continued excitedly. "I think we have a tape somewhere—"

"*No* we *don't*," Mr. Baxter said firmly.

Cory's ears perked up. He could actually hear the stress in his father's voice. That could only mean one thing: P.P.E., Potential Parental Embarrassment. *Now* I'm interested, he thought.

"I've got to see that tape," Cory told his father.

"*No* you *don't*," Mr. Baxter repeated.

"Hey, we're back!" exclaimed the pretty announcer on *Undercover Superstar*. "So let's meet the superstars our undercover talent scouts discovered at schools just like yours. . . ."

Raven's family stared at the TV screen, eager to see this week's contestants. Raven found herself staring at the screen, too, but she wasn't watching the show any longer. . . .